ON TOP OF THE WORLD

For Melissa

A Red Fox Book

Published by Random House Children's Books
20 Vauxhall Bridge Road, London SW1V 2SA

A division of The Random House Group Ltd
London Melbourne Sydney Auckland
Johannesburg and agencies throughout the world

1 3 5 7 9 10 8 6 4 2

First published in Great Britain by The Bodley Head Children's Books 1998

Red Fox edition 2001

Printed and bound in Singapore

THE RANDOM HOUSE GROUP Limited Reg. No. 954009

www.randomhouse.co.uk

ISBN 0 09 926284 3

ON TOP OF THE WORLD

JOHN PRATER

RED FOX

Once a year, on a
warm summer night
when the moon is full,
all toys everywhere
leave their owners for
a night of fun.

Bear, Rabbit, Mimi and Peep felt very excited.

'I haven't done this before,' said Bear.

'Nor have we,' said Mimi and Peep.

'Well, I have,' said Rabbit, 'and it's great!'

'Here we are,' said
Rabbit.
'What is it?' asked
Peep.
'Looks like a very big
step,' said Bear.
They climbed up.

'Oh, look, another one,' said Mimi. 'Yes,' said Rabbit, 'there are many more, and when we have climbed them all we will be on top of the world!'

Up and up they
climbed...

and up some more...

until, at last, as night
became day, they
found themselves
on top of the world!

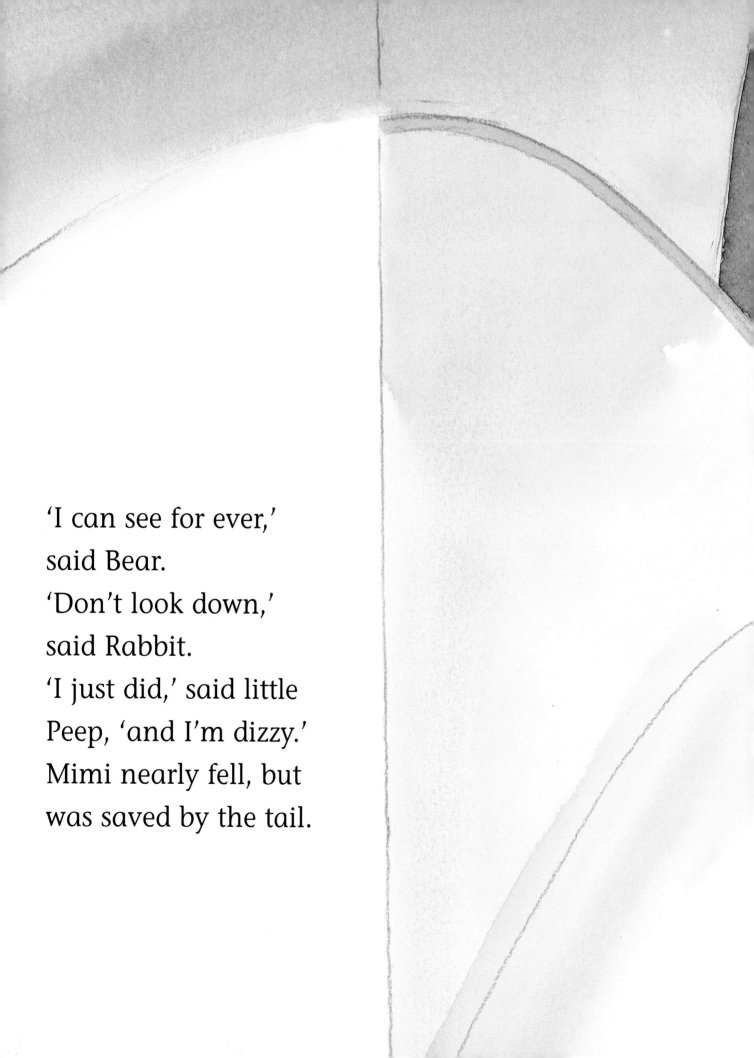

'I can see for ever,'
said Bear.
'Don't look down,'
said Rabbit.
'I just did,' said little
Peep, 'and I'm dizzy.'
Mimi nearly fell, but
was saved by the tail.

'Now let's get ready
for the best bit,' said
Rabbit.
A ray of sun bathed
the slide in golden
light.
'Ready?'
asked Rabbit.
    'Steady?
        Go!'

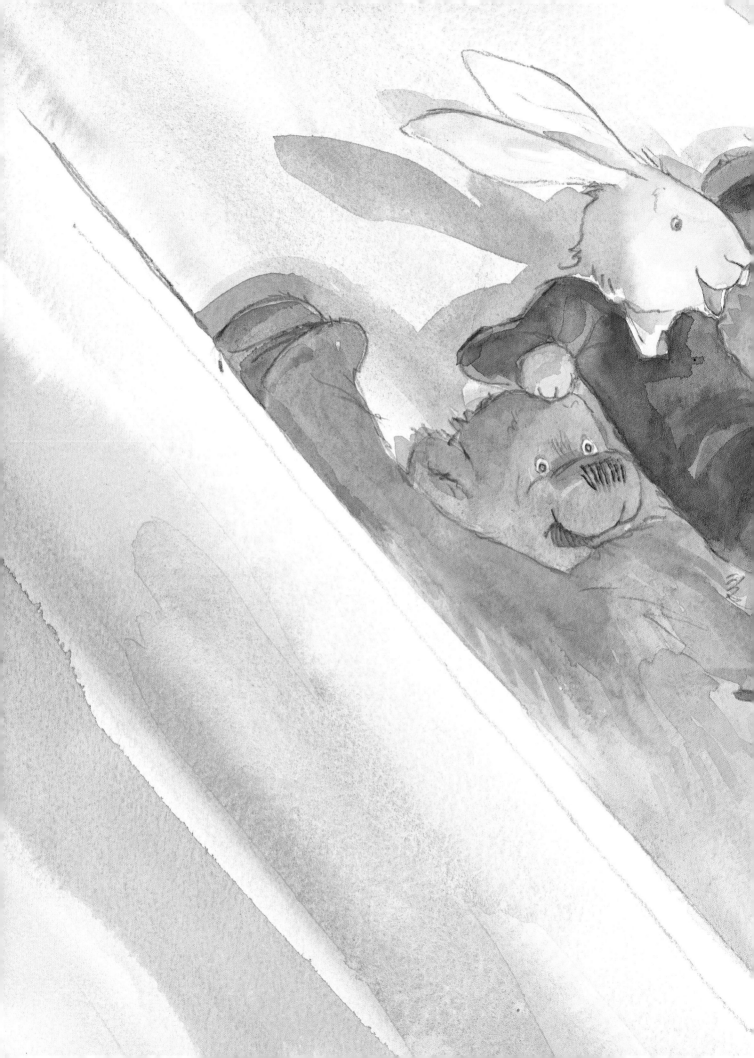

'Wow!' said Peep.
'Let's do it again.'
But there was no
time left.
Perhaps next year,
one warm,
moonlit
night....

More Red Fox picture books
for you to enjoy

ELMER
by David McKee 0099697203

MUMMY LAID AN EGG
by Babette Cole 0099299119

RUNAWAY TRAIN
by Benedict Blathwayt 0099385716

DOGGER
by Shirley Hughes 009992790X

WHERE THE WILD THINGS ARE
by Maurice Sendak 0099408392

OLD BEAR
by Jane Hissey 0099265761

MISTER MAGNOLIA
by Quentin Blake 0099400421

ALFIE GETS IN FIRST
by Shirley Hughes 0099855607

OI! GET OFF OUR TRAIN
by John Burningham 009985340X

GORGEOUS
by Caroline Castle and Sam Childs 0099400766